If Only I Were...

written and illustrated

by

Mary Mitchell Tartaglia

ONEWORLD BOOKS FOR CHILDREN

Just off the path between the farmhouse and the barn was a very big oak tree. He was the biggest, the strongest, the happiest oak tree on the farm. Farmer Basil always called him "Smiley".

Smiley was a very useful tree. The children made a swing on one of his branches. They climbed on Smiley too, and when they were tired they took a nap resting against his big, gnarled trunk.

In the summer when it was very hot, the neighbors played horseshoes in the shade of Smiley's branches. The whole family would take time out from their work to enjoy the shade and a good game.

In the winter when it was shivering cold Smiley spread his branches to protect the house from the bitter wind. Farmer Basil always remembered to thank Smiley with a little pat on his trunk.

On the other side of the path grew a very scrawny tree. Scrawny was only four years old. More than anything she wanted to be big. BIG and STRONG and TALL, with lots of leaves and deep roots just like Smiley.

"Oh, poor me," you could hear Scrawny say. "No-one can play horseshoes in my shade, I'm too small; and a swing would surely break me in two, my branches are so thin. And last year, when it was bitterly cold, I shook so hard, BRR BRR, one of my branches broke in two. Oh, woe is me to be born a scrawny tree."

Scrawny grew sadder and sadder. One day Farmer Basil strode up to her carrying what looked like a huge pair of scissors. He started snipping away at the tips of her branches. Scrawny was sure she was being cut up for firewood. "I'm good for nothing," she thought miserably. "Nothing but firewood." But Farmer Basil smiled and said, "Just wait and see."

In the spring, Farmer Basil raked away the leaves near Scrawny and there underneath were rows of tiny green plants. "At last!" thought Scrawny, "here is something smaller than me!" Then Farmer Basil bent down to one of the little plants and said, "What fine strawberries we'll have from you this year."

Scrawny almost screamed. "That . . . that tiny, creepy plant makes STRAWBERRIES?" she spluttered. "I'm bigger than he is and *I* can't make strawberries. Oh, woe is me to be born a scrawny tree." And before long, all the strawberries were big and ripe and the field was full of happy people filling their baskets with the sweet, red fruit.

All through the summer, Scrawny watched the other plants growing around her. "Why can't I be a strawberry plant, or even rhubarb?" she wondered unhappily. "Carrots can't be difficult to make, or tomatoes. And the corn seems to be growing right up to the sky!" But Scrawny was so busy wishing she was something she wasn't that she never noticed she too was CHANGING.

Autumn came and all the crops were ready to harvest. Scrawny felt more miserable than ever. When Farmer Basil came down the path carrying a very big basket in his arms, poor Scrawny shivered with fright. "I'm going to be chopped into firewood, I know it – FIREWOOD!" she squealed.

But no! Farmer Basil patted her on her scrawny trunk and said proudly, "What a lovely, generous tree you are! Why, I've never seen so many juicy apples." Scrawny wiped the tears from her eyes and squeaked, "Apples? Did he say apples?"

And for the very first time, Scrawny looked carefully at her own branches. What a surprise! What a delight! For there she saw APPLES, big, red, juicy, lovely apples. "I'm an apple tree!" she cried, and nearly jumped right out of the ground in delight.

Soon everyone was filling baskets to the brim and talking about all the lovely pies they would make. And if you had listened very carefully, you could have heard Scrawny singing to herself, "Oh lucky me, for I was born an apple tree!"

To Mom with love

Oneworld Publications Ltd
(Sales and Editorial)
185 Banbury Road
Oxford OX2 7AR
England

Oneworld Publications Ltd
(U.S. Sales Office)
County Route 9
P.O. Box 357
Chatham, NY 12037, U.S.A.

If Only I Were . . .
© Text & illustrations Mary Mitchell Tartaglia 1993
All rights reserved. Copyright under Berne Convention

ISBN 1-85168-038-1
Printed and bound by Tien Wah Press, Singapore